BRITANNICA BEGINNER BIOS

LEONARDO DA VINCI
GENIUS OF THE ITALIAN RENAISSANCE

JUSTINE CIOVACCO

Britannica
Educational Publishing

IN ASSOCIATION WITH

ROSEN
EDUCATIONAL SERVICES

Published in 2015 by Britannica Educational Publishing (a trademark of Encyclopædia Britannica, Inc.) in association with The Rosen Publishing Group, Inc.
29 East 21st Street, New York, NY 10010

Distributed exclusively by Rosen Publishing.
To see additional Britannica Educational Publishing titles, go to rosenpublishing.com.

First Edition

Britannica Educational Publishing
J. E. Luebering: Director, Core Reference Group
Mary Rose McCudden: Editor, Britannica Student Encyclopedia

Rosen Publishing
Hope Lourie Killcoyne: Executive Editor
Tracey Baptiste: Editor
Nelson Sá: Art Director
Brian Garvey: Designer
Cindy Reiman: Photography Manager
Karen Huang: Photo Researcher

Library of Congress Cataloging-in-Publication Data

Ciovacco, Justine.
Leonardo da Vinci/Justine Ciovacco.—First Edition.
pages cm.—(Britannica beginner bios)
Includes bibliographical references and index.
ISBN 978-1-62275-677-3 (library bound) — ISBN 978-1-62275-678-0 (pbk.) —
ISBN 978-1-62275-679-7 (6-pack)
1. Leonardo, da Vinci, 1452–1519—Juvenile literature. 2. Artists—Italy—Biography—Juvenile literature. 3. Scientists—Italy—Biography—Juvenile literature. I. Title.
N6923.L33C52 2014
709.2—dc23

[B]
    2014013945

Manufactured in the United States of America

CONTENTS

CHAPTER ONE

WHO WAS LEONARDO DA VINCI?

Many people can do one thing well. Some people can do many things well. Leonardo da Vinci was a person who was good at many things. He was a talented artist who created paintings, drawings, and sculptures. He was also a great mind in the field of science.

Leonardo da Vinci is one of the world's most famous artists.

Leonardo lived in Italy in the 1400s during a period of time called the Renaissance. The word *Renaissance* means "rebirth" in French. It was called this because there was a rebirth of interest in ancient Greece and Rome. The Europeans of the Renaissance took the ideas of the ancient people and built on these ideas to develop their own. The work of artists became more true to

Leonardo's painting of John the Baptist now hangs in the Louvre museum in Paris.

life. They designed beautiful buildings. They made colorful paintings. They carved SCULPTURES of important people. Artists, scientists, and inventors were encouraged in their work. It was a time when new ideas had a chance to grow.

The Renaissance was also a time when people began to invent machines that changed the way people lived and worked. For example, the printing press was a new machine that made it easier to print books.

Leonardo stood out as one of Italy's greatest artists of the Renaissance period. His style of painting was unlike any other artist. Today, his

Vocabulary Box

SCULPTURES are pieces of art usually made by carving clay, metal, or stone.

Quick Fact

Other famous artists of the Renaissance period are Michelangelo and Raphael.

The *Mona Lisa* always attracts a big crowd of visitors to the Louvre.

works the *Mona Lisa* and *The Last Supper* are two of the world's most famous paintings.

But Leonardo was much more than just a painter. He studied many different subjects and was talented in all of them. Today, someone like that is known as a Renaissance man. Leonardo watched humans and animals and made drawings to show how they moved.

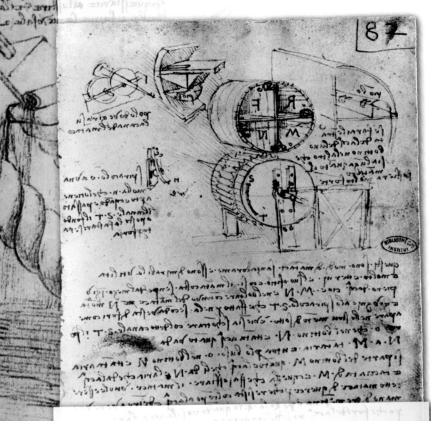

Leonardo made sketches and notes in notebooks before creating artwork.

He was an inventor, too. He loved to draw and build things. Leonardo thought about all kinds of new machines. He drew plans for a flying machine more than 400 years before the first airplane was built. He recorded his ideas in many notebooks. Today, those notebooks and his artwork show his great talent. In modern times, people have built machines using the designs in his notebooks. His plans were so good that some of the machines actually work!

CHAPTER TWO

EARLY LIFE

Leonardo da Vinci was born on April 15, 1452. His family lived in a village called Anchiano in what is now Italy. The nearest town was Vinci. That is how he got his name. His full name means "Leonardo of Vinci" in Italian.

Vinci is still covered by rolling, grassy hills, like it was in Leonardo's time.

Quick Fact

Vinci is about 20 miles (32 kilometers) from Florence.

9

Leonardo's father was named Ser Piero. He was a lawyer and a landlord. Leonardo's mother was named Caterina. She was young and poor. Leonardo was raised mostly by his father's parents and his Uncle Francesco.

His family made sure that he was taught reading, writing, and arithmetic. Leonardo taught himself many other subjects later in life.

Leonardo spent a great deal of time with his Uncle Francesco. Francesco was a farmer. He took Leonardo on walks around Vinci. He showed his nephew the beauty of **NATURE**. Vinci had many hills, olive

The Virgin and Child with Saint Anne is one of Leonardo's paintings with a beautiful, natural background.

Vocabulary Box

NATURE is the world around us that is not made by people. Plants, animals, the sky, and the oceans are all part of nature.

Even Leonardo's sketches of flowers look like they pop off the page.

trees, and gardens. It was a good place to enjoy nature.

Leonardo loved the colors of leaves and flowers. He studied how water moved. He saw how things looked different in and out of sunlight. He drew everything he saw. Leonardo's love of nature showed in his art and other creations. His detailed drawings helped make all of the natural objects in his paintings look as if they were real.

CHAPTER THREE

AN ARTIST'S BEGINNING

Ser Piero knew that his son was talented. When Leonardo was about 15 years old, Ser Piero arranged for him to study painting in the city of Florence. Leonardo helped the artist Andrea del Verrocchio in his studio. Verrocchio taught Leonardo many skills, such as how to draw,

Andrea Verrocchio was a talented artist who taught Leonardo many things.

paint, and sculpt. Leonardo also learned metalwork, carpentry, and leather arts. Verrocchio also helped him study how devices worked.

Leonardo painted an angel in Verrocchio's painting the *Baptism of Christ*. To some people, the angel was painted perfectly. The buyer of the painting loved the angel more than anything else. According to one story,

Leonardo also painted an angel in *The Annunciation*.

Verrocchio was so impressed with Leonardo's angel that he vowed never to paint again. Leonardo became a member of Florence's painters' guild in 1472. This meant he was accepted as a professional artist at age 20. However, Leonardo continued to work in his teacher's workshop for five more years.

Leonardo was popular with many **PATRONS**. They had a lot of money to spend on artwork, and they wanted Leonardo to make art for them. In 1482, Leonardo moved to Milan. He went to work for Ludovico Sforza, who was a duke and the ruler of the city. Leonardo spent 17 years in Milan. He had his own workshop and students. Some of his students became famous painters themselves. During his time in Milan, he is said to have finished six paintings for the duke. However, three of those paintings have been lost.

Vocabulary Box
PATRONS are people who give money to support an artist's work.

Sforza also wanted Leonardo to make a horse sculpture to honor his dead father. Leonardo made a clay model of a horse. It was more than 20 feet tall! Leonardo spent more than 10 years building the horse. He planned to make a final horse in bronze, but he never did. Milan was at war and bronze was needed to make cannons.

This plan was like many of Leonardo's projects. He was a great dreamer, but he could

Leonardo made detailed sketches for the animals in *St. George and the Dragon*.

In this reproduction of Leonardo's *The Last Supper,* Jesus is seated at the center.

not always finish his work. He took a lot of time. He would step back and look at each detail. He would study the science of what he did. Leonardo wanted his work to be perfect.

Quick Fact

Leonardo painted the table and dishes in *Th Last Supper* to look like the ones in the monks' dining hall.

Leonardo did finish one of his most famous works during this period, however. From 1495 to 1498, he made a painting on a wall in a dining hall used by Christian monks. The painting was called *The Last Supper*. It shows an important event in the story of **CHRISTIANITY**. People have always loved the beauty of the painting and how real the men look.

> **Vocabulary Box**
> **CHRISTIANITY** is a religion that started about 2,000 years ago. It is based on the life, death, and teachings of a man named Jesus.

Unfortunately, not much of the original painting remains today. It has faded and crumbled with time. However, it was restored in the late 1900s and can still be seen in the dining hall. There are also many copies of the painting. Some were made by Leonardo's assistants.

CHAPTER FOUR

LEONARDO'S NOTEBOOKS

I n Milan, Leonardo started to think more about science. He realized that knowing how things worked would make him a better artist, scientist, and inventor. Leonardo still loved painting and drawing, but

Some people make models based on Leonardo's sketches. This is based on the sketch of a tank.

he wanted to design more things.

He drew everything in notebooks. He would **SKETCH** ideas for paintings and things he saw in nature. He would dream of beautiful buildings and machines that could do new things. He watched birds fly and wanted to do the same. He drew plans for flying machines and the pieces needed to make them fly.

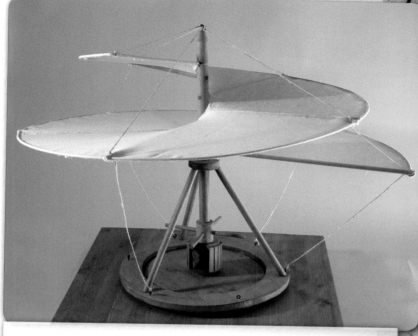

This model is based on one of Leonardo's sketches of a part for a flying machine.

One odd fact about Leonardo's notebooks is that he wrote them using "mirror writing." Mirror writing reads from right to left, which is how normal writing would look in a mirror. Some people think he did this because he was left-handed and did not want to smudge his writing. Others think he wanted to make it hard for people to take his ideas.

In 1503, Leonardo returned to Florence. He was welcomed to the city as a famous artist. But he was also known for his other interests. He was hired as an expert in **ARCHITECTURE** to find out

Leonardo used tiny, backward writing in all of his notebooks.

why a church in Florence had been damaged. He also worked in the military, sketching plans and creating maps of cities. Leonardo even drew up plans to change the course of a river that ran behind the city of Pisa. Although he was not successful, this led to another plan to build a water canal that would connect Florence to the sea. The plans were never carried out, but centuries later, a highway was built in the same place Leonardo had chosen for his canal. Leonardo also spent a lot of time in hospitals studying the human body. There are many sketches of parts of the body in his notebooks.

Vocabulary Box

ARCHITECTURE is the art and science of planning and creating buildings.

Quick Fact

Leonardo's notebooks show the many different things he thought about. His subjects included buildings, clothing, math problems, plants, musical instruments, weapons, and lists of words.

21

CHAPTER FIVE

THE *MONA LISA*

In Florence, Leonardo worked on some of his greatest paintings. One was the *Mona Lisa*. This is probably his most popular painting today.

The *Mona Lisa* is a portrait of a woman. For many centuries, no one knew who the woman in the *Mona Lisa* was. Experts now think that she may have been Lisa Gherardini, the wife of a merchant from Florence. The merchant's last name was Gioconda, so the painting is sometimes called *La Gioconda*. The painting is mysterious in other ways, too. The woman in the

Vocabulary Box

A GENIUS is a very smart or talented person.

For hundreds of years, people have wondered who *Mona Lisa* is and why she has a slight smile.

painting seems to be smiling. But many people have wondered about her expression. No one knows exactly what it means. This is Leonardo's **GENIUS**. His artwork looks so real that it makes people care about who or what is in them.

The *Mona Lisa* draws

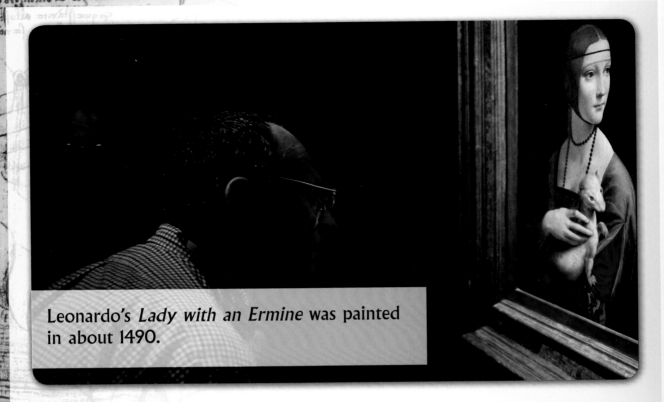

Leonardo's *Lady with an Ermine* was painted in about 1490.

Quick Fact

The *Mona Lisa* is now on display in the Louvre, a museum in Paris, France.

thousands of visitors to the Louvre every year. The painting was stolen once, but it was recovered two years later. It is now displayed behind protective glass.

CHAPTER SIX

LEONARDO'S FINAL YEARS

Leonardo returned to Milan in 1506. In 1513, he moved to Rome. Many other famous artists were working in Rome at that time, but Leonardo stayed only three years. In 1516, Leonardo moved to Cloux (now Clos-Lucé), France. He was there to work for King Francis I of France. His title was "First painter, architect, and ENGINEER to the King." The king paid Leonardo to do anything the artist wanted. Leonardo

Vocabulary Box

An **ENGINEER** is someone who uses science and math to design and build useful machines and structures.

25

spent much of his time in France editing his writings. For the king, he drew plans for a palace and garden. He also made sketches for court festivals. Otherwise, the king left him alone and treated him as an honored guest.

Leonardo died in Cloux on May 2, 1519. He was buried in the palace church of Saint-Florentin. The

This painting by another artist shows a sick Leonardo in bed speaking with King Francis I.

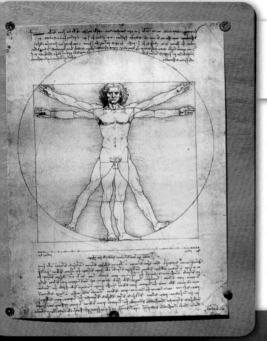

This is a drawing of the human body from one of Leonardo's notebooks.

church was torn down in the early 1800s. Leonardo's grave can no longer be found. His paintings and notebooks are still studied and enjoyed by millions of people around the world.

Quick Fact

A museum in Florence has models of some of the machines that Leonardo sketched in his notebooks.

A leather-covered book of Leonardo's sketches is pictured. It holds 600 drawings of the human body, including one of his most famous (*above*).

TIMELINE

1452: Leonardo is born on April 15 in Anchiano, near Vinci, in what is now Italy.

1473: Leonardo makes his first known drawing, *Landscape Drawing of the Arno Valley*.

about 1470–75: Leonardo paints *The Annunciation* and helps Verrocchio paint the *Baptism of Christ*.

about 1474–78: Leonardo paints a portrait of Ginevra de' Benci.

1481: Leonardo begins painting *Adoration of the Magi*. It is unfinished.

1482: Leonardo leaves Florence to work in Milan for Duke Ludovico Sforza.

1483: Leonardo begins painting *Virgin of the Rocks* along with two younger artists.

1489–90: Leonardo paints *Lady with an Ermine*.

1490: Leonardo designs sets and costumes for *Il Paradiso* (also called *The Feast of Paradise*), a play put on at the wedding feast of the duke's nephew.

1491: Leonardo designs clothing for the duke's wedding.

1498: Leonardo finishes *The Last Supper*.

about 1499: Leonardo draws a life-size sketch called *Virgin and Child with St. Anne and the Young St. John the Baptist*.

1502–16: Leonardo works on *Virgin and Child with St. Anne*, but it remains unfinished.

about 1503–06: In Florence, Leonardo paints the *Mona Lisa*.

1506–08: Leonardo paints a second version of *Virgin of the Rocks*.

about 1510: Leonardo draws his self-portrait in red chalk.

1516: Leonardo moves to Cloux (now Clos-Lucé), France, to work for King Francis I. He paints his final painting, a portrait of Saint John the Baptist.

1519: Leonardo dies on May 2 at age 67. He leaves his notebooks and paintings to his friend and student, Francesco Melzi.

GLOSSARY

DESIGN To make something according to plan.

DETAIL A small part of something larger.

DEVICES Objects, machines, or tools made for a special purpose or to do a job.

DUKE A man of high rank in the highest class of society; dukes tend to have great riches and power.

INVENTOR A person who creates or makes new things.

LIFETIME The whole life of a person, from birth to death.

MODEL A pattern of something to be made; a model may be made of a larger piece of artwork so that the artist can plan his or her work; also, a small copy of an object based on a sketch or design.

MONKS Men who live and work in a religious community.

PROFESSIONAL Someone who is paid for his or her work.

STUDIO A building or room where an artist works.

TALENTED Naturally able to do something well.

BOOKS

Barretta, Gene. *Neo Leo: The Ageless Ideas of Leonardo da Vinci*. New York, NY: Henry Holt and Co., 2009.

Langley, Andrew. *DK Eyewitness Books: Da Vinci and His Times*. New York, NY: DK Eyewitness Books, 2006.

Phillips, John. *Leonardo da Vinci: The Genius Who Defined the Renaissance*. Washington, DC: National Geographic Kids, 2008.

Wood, Alix. *Artists Through the Ages: Leonardo da Vinci*. New York, NY: Windmill Books, 2013.

WEBSITES

Because of the changing nature of Internet links, Rosen Publishing has developed an online list of websites related to the subject of this book. This site is updated regularly. Please use this link to access the list:

http://www.rosenlinks.com/BBB/Vinci

INDEX